BORN OF RAGE

THE LEAGUE
NEMESIS RISING

SHERRILYN
KENYON

OLIVER
HEBER
BOOKS

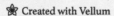 Created with Vellum

For my brothers.

Strong Alone. Stronger Together.

—Sanctum Sentella

BORN OF RAGE

SHERRILYN KENYON

Death had taken her entire family from her when she was just a girl, and now that relentless bastard was back, coming for her.

Stalking her.

Dakari Tievel could feel its fetid breath on her neck as she rushed through the dark shadows of the vacant alley of this godforsaken outpost, trying her best to elude its hateful agents.

She shivered. Not from fear, as she'd come to terms with the inevitability of death long ago. Honestly, she was more than ready to be with her brother and parents again. She'd more than welcome that long overdue reunion.

Rather her tremors came from the frigid cold that had taken all the sensation from her fingertips, while she searched desperately for the address she'd been given by one of her former guards.

These people will help you, my lady. It's what they do.

Dakari wasn't sure if she believed in heroes anymore. Not of any kind. In this day and age, they were in short supply. Those who were willing to stand up for others and risk their lives . . . they were the stuff of childhood dreams.

Most were too absorbed with their own suffering to care about anyone else's. She'd learned that when she was six and the people of her world had stood aside and let her family be slaughtered for no reason whatsoever.

Then they'd embraced their killer without bothering to see him punished for his cruelty and crimes. It sickened her to this day that people could be so blind. So mean.

So unfeeling.

But no one had cared. No one had stood up and said, *this is wrong!* The guilty should be punished!

Instead, they'd gone on with their lives, knowing what had been done to her and her family was deplorable. Telling her that they were sorry about it. That one day, she'd rise above it and move it. But no one had spoken up or helped. They'd turned their gazes away in fear of that same injustice coming for them with the same ruthless vengeance that it used to lay her family low for no reason whatsoever.

Their callous apathy was what had caused the deep, dark void in her soul that had never healed. Too early in life, she'd learned the truth of others.

Everyone was selfish. Only out for themselves.

People would only help when they had something to gain. Either a warm, fuzzy feeling in their belly or applause from those around them.

No one helped because it was the right thing to do. And that included the guard who'd given her this address. Why would he do anything for no reason, at all?

She should have known better.

"I'm a fool for being here."

In her heart, she believed that. No one had ever once helped her. Why would they start now?

Most likely, this was a fabricated address. The

guard had probably sent her to her death. Just for shits and giggles.

Like everyone else in her life.

Torture the little girl. Watch her suffer. It was what people liked to do for entertainment.

For some reason, watching the misery of others seemed to make them feel better about their own pathetic lives. Especially when they thought the person being harmed had something better than them or that they were somehow "blessed."

But she'd never been blessed. Dakari had been cursed from the moment of birth.

In spite of her "royal" birth, she had risked her life to leave her home. It'd taken every last cred to her name to get here. She'd barely escaped the last assassin who'd been sent to kill her. If these people turned her away . . .

Don't think about it.

Right now, she couldn't afford to let her panic override what little courage she had left.

Breathe, Dakaboo. Just breathe. I'm right here with you. I'll always be with you. Tears filled her eyes as she heard her brother's voice in her head, whispering the comforting words he'd said to her the night they'd slaughtered their parents.

The night they'd divided them.

Barely six, she'd screamed and kicked, clawing at the soldiers as they brutally pulled her from her brother's arms. That pain still choked her. Still burned so raw inside at times that she wondered how she'd managed to remain sane.

That night had been so unreal. So traumatic.

For everyone.

Unlike her, her brother had seen their parents' die. Had witnessed the carnage up close and personal.

Then, terrified that he would be next and determined to save Dakari's life, he'd come to her bed and wrapped her in a blanket. "We have to go, Dakari."

Five years older, Jinx had still been a kid himself. Yet he'd managed to stay strong and calm through the coup that had claimed the lives of everyone they loved.

He'd covered her head to keep her from seeing the bodies or blood, but the screams of that night were forever seared into her memory. As was the sound of his strong, steady heartbeat as he carried her through their home to what he'd prayed was safety.

"It'll be all right. I'm right here. I'll never let you go." Words whispered over and over until he'd made it to the hangar bay only to discover it'd been their own half-brother who had torn their lives apart.

Tobin had been waiting in the hangar bay with more soldiers, to cut off Jinx's escape.

Greedy, selfish, rotten piece of shit. Spoiled beyond spoiled, Tobin had no reason to harm them or their parents. He'd lived a lavish, carefree life.

It hadn't been enough.

He'd wanted everything that wasn't his.

Even if it meant killing them all to have it.

Now on this cold outpost, Dakari stumbled as the rage and pain washed over her anew. She still wanted his heart in her fist. To this day, she couldn't understand why he'd spared her when he'd spared no one else his wrath. Not that Tobin hadn't tried to brainwash her with his lies and excuses. Gaslight her into believing she hadn't seen what she'd seen.

Or heard the truth with her own ears.

"I was there to rescue you, Dakari. You were too young to remember it! That was not how it happened at all. I saved you! Not Jinx. He died with your parents."

Lying bastard!

As if she could ever forget her real brother's kindness and care. What it felt like to really be loved.

Like she didn't know the difference between a hero and a coward.

And now because she wouldn't fall in line and do what he wanted, Tobin had sicced the League that governed all their worlds on her with the worst sort of kill orders imaginable.

Thrill-Kill.

It wasn't just enough to kill her. The assassins were to tear her apart and make an example of her for others.

Just like Tobin had ordered for their father and her mother.

Just like he'd done to Jinx.

There was no justice in this universe that was ruled by the League and the monsters it created that preyed on all of them. She knew that better than anyone.

Damn them for it!

"Careful, love. Watch where you're going!"

Dakari bit back a scream as that unexpected voice intruded on her thoughts. Until she realized that the man speaking wasn't one of the assassins hunting her.

He was . . .

Huge!

And intimidating. But at least this one wasn't trying to cut off her head or stab her.

So, she forced herself to smile at him and act as normal as she could manage given her near frantic state. "Is this the *Hunting Ground*?" Her guard had told her to go to that dingy bar on the inhospitable Trigange Outpost where her would-be saviors often hung out during their off-hours.

If they weren't there when she arrived, the owner of the place would know how to reach them and would offer her protection until they could find her.

Although why she was putting her faith in such a long shot, she had no idea. That alone, spoke tomes of just how desperate her plight had become. Trust was as alien a concept to her as bathing appeared to be for the bald, purple-skinned man in front of her.

His gaze narrowed with suspicion. Then, faster than she could blink, he pulled out a blaster and angled it at her head.

Breathless, she didn't have time to react before he pulled the trigger and shot.

Only instead of blasting her head from her shoulders, he shot barely an inch past her cheek, into the darkness.

"Damn assassins. Like cockroaches. See one, there's a dozen you don't." Spitting on the ground at his feet, he holstered his weapon. "You the target?"

"I . . ." Dakari hesitated to answer as the truth could very well get her killed. The bounty on her life was staggering. "I'm looking for Eve Itxara. I was told she comes here a lot."

He ignored her. "How much is your life worth?"

"Yours, if you don't move along."

Dakari gasped at the sound of a deep, sultry voice so close to her ear that if the woman had meant her harm, she'd be dead already. How had she gotten that close to her without her knowing it? All these months of living on edge, of being hyper-vigilant to every single sound and vibration, no one had gotten the drop on her like this.

No one.

Except for this woman.

"Who are you?"

She stepped out of the shadows with a sly, wicked grin. Tall and lean with lush dark skin, she had the kind of athletic build that said she could hold her own with anyone. And while there were no weapons apparent on the woman's body, Dakari had no doubt she was lethal. Every part of her bearing said she was honed for battle and ready to take on anything the League or anyone else threw at her.

Eve of Destruction was just what Dakari had been promised.

Just what she needed.

From the top of her long, Andarion braids to the bottom of her high-heeled lace boots. Damn! What Dakari wouldn't give to look so intimidating and bad-ass.

The man held his hands up and took a step back. "C'mon, Eve. No need to be like that."

She smirked. "No need, but ridding the galaxy of assholes is my sole form of entertainment, Bailey."

He bolted so fast that Dakari was surprised he didn't leave a wet trail in his wake.

"Nice."

"Not really. Most refer to me as a raging, hormonal bitch." Eve rolled her shoulders which caused the leather of her black jacket to creak in protest. "Personally, I take that as a compliment."

"You would."

Dakari's breath caught as she realized Eve wasn't alone. Turning sharply, she saw another woman behind her. One similar enough in looks that it marked them as family. Only this one had long black hair that was held back from her face in a severe ponytail. Her unblemished skin was much paler than Eve's, but she was no less bad-ass and fierce.

The woman glanced down the alley. "Did you take care of our friend, Jedi?"

"No shit, Jayne." The masculine voice rumbled out of the darkness like thunder. "Bastard's napping."

Jayne smirked. "Dirt?"

"Any other kind for his low species?"

"Good man." Eve pulled out a pair of sunglasses and covered her copper-colored eyes with them. "Come along, Dakari Tievel. We need to chat."

Stunned on multiple levels, Dakari watched as an insanely tall man approached them. With a head full of long, dark, riotous curls, he was unbelievably handsome. And his swagger said that he was more than aware of it. That he'd probably conquered every heterosexual female who'd ever crossed his path.

Well-muscled and sporting enough weapons to double as an assault vehicle on his own, he winked at her, then turned toward Eve. "Hey, boss lady? I don't want to argue what you're doing, because I'm not stupid, but since when do we interfere with League contracts? I mean . . . that was a League assassin you just had me take out, right? And last time I checked that shit'll get you killed in any galaxy, anywhere, any time."

Jayne scoffed at his question. "You turning craven, Tweed?"

"No. But I'm not suicidal either."

Eve arched a brow at him.

"Fair point, given some of my more recent actions and proclivity for reckless drinking." He scratched at his jaw. "However, dodging League checkpoints and skirting laws is one thing. All-out war on their assassins . . . I like having my body parts where the gods meant them to be, you know? And I really like my head on top of my shoulders."

Eve folded her arms over her chest. "Then maybe we ought to get off the street and out of sight, huh?"

Speaking in another language that Dakari couldn't understand, Jedi rolled his eyes.

Jayne clapped him on the back. "Don't lip my sister, pirate. Remember, she bites."

He snorted at her warning. "Like I don't have the bitemarks all over my ass to prove it?" He raked a disgruntled smirk over the attractive woman's body. "Why do I like you again, Jayne?"

She held her hands up to accentuate her rugged clothing. "My daring fashion sense."

"More like, my severe head injury."

Jayne laughed.

Eve groaned at their play. "And you're both about to get an ass-beating if you don't stop and move out."

Jedi saluted her. "Yes, my mistress and tormenter."

"Are you related to them, too?" Dakari asked him as he led her toward a transport.

With a confused scowl, Jedi shook his head. "No. Why?"

For one thing, she couldn't imagine a man his size allowing someone to talk to him like that unless they were related. Secondly . . . "You argue with them the way I used to with my brother."

A peculiar air came over Eve before she offered her a smile. "We might not be blood, but we're family just the same. It's why I tolerate his gargantuan ass and his bad attitude."

"Not to mention, my bad driving." He flashed a wicked grin at her before he rushed to take up the driver's seat.

Eve started to argue, then appeared to surrender

the fight as he strapped himself in. "Fine. Just get us back to the *Remorseless* in one piece, Jedidiah."

No sooner had she spoken than light exploded around them. Followed by heavy blaster fire.

Cursing as Jayne returned fire and Jedi jumped back out of the transport to help, Eve pulled a blaster from beneath her jacket. "I thought you neutralized that assassin."

Jedi grimaced as he shielded Dakari with his body. "Apparently he had friends."

Angry friends by the looks and sounds of it. No sooner had Jedi pulled her clear of the transport than it exploded.

Terrified, Dakari shrank back as shrapnel rained down around them.

Eve took her arm and pulled her toward another alley while Jedi covered their retreat.

"How many?" Jayne asked.

"Six. Nine. Twenty dozen. Hell, if I can tell."

"Follow me!" Eve tossed a grenade toward their enemies, then ran down the dark alley with such ease that Dakari couldn't fathom it, unless her glasses had some kind of infrared in them.

After a few minutes and more rounds of fire, she kicked open a door and pulled Dakari through it.

"Where are going?"

Jedi snorted. "So long as it avoids death or custody, do you care?"

"Not really."

"Then, shut-up and follow." Eve urged her in front while she fired off a round to cover Jedi's and Jayne's retreat.

Dakari kept running forward, through the vacant, rundown building with no destination, other than to avoid death and whatever nightmare was in pursuit of them. But unlike Eve, she wasn't graceful about it as she tripped and fell against things in the dark.

She turned left and slammed into something solid. Real solid and yet . . .

Terror consumed her as she realized it was a man.

No. Not a man.

An assassin.

The kind they were doing their best to avoid. Shit!

He reacted instantly. Grabbing Dakari before she could think to protest or even scream, he shoved her into a closet, then pushed Eve, Jayne and Jedi in on top of her and locked it.

Panicking and confused, she expected them to fight or curse. Do something.

Anything.

Instead, they motioned for her to be quiet as they took up positions in the small room and holstered their weapons. Completely baffled, she listened to the sounds outside as their pursuers caught up to their location.

"Damn it! Where'd they go?"

"They must have veered off before they came this way." The man's voice was calm and heavily accented.

"I saw them come in here!"

"You must have been mistaken. I've been here the whole time. No one entered before you."

"But—"

"Want to keep arguing with a Top Ass or you want to find your target, Agent?"

"Sorry, sir." He rushed off.

Even more perplexed by it all, Dakari frowned at the delighted look on Eve's face, especially given the next words they heard that didn't detract from that happy expression at all. "High Commander Shadowborne. Building one, clear. If the subs head this way, I'll take them down with extreme prejudice."

If that was the assassin's intentions, then why were Eve and Jayne smiling while Jedi smirked? Why bother to hide them when he intended to kill them?

None of this made any sense.

Why were her "protectors" so comfortable with a League assassin standing just outside the door, talking to his colleagues about their murders? The League wasn't exactly known for using soldiers or agents other than its own military personnel.

Charged with keeping the peace over all the existing worlds and outposts, they were their own legal system that controlled everyone with an iron fist. No government was safe from them.

Their assassins were judge and jury for anyone stupid enough to get in their way, especially when someone, like her, had a kill-warrant issued against their life. Then anyone around them was deemed an acceptable loss. No assassin could get into trouble for taking out what they deemed collateral damage. Being around someone they wanted dead was *your* mistake.

No one would care.

There wasn't even anyone to complain to.

That man standing outside could do anything he wanted to all of them and no one would be able to stop him. So why were the others so calm and nonchalant?

Her answer came a few minutes later when the door slid open and the assassin tsked at them. "One simple task, Evara. Is that too much to ask?"

Arms akimbo, Eve walked seductively toward him. "You're a fine one to talk, given the number of times I've saved your cute little ass. I do believe you still owe me."

Against all League rules and protocol, a smile broke across his handsome face. "Always, *mi amita*." Pulling her against him, he kissed her.

Dakari was so stunned that it took her a second to realize that the assassin had spoken his endearment in Euforian. *My dearest.* It'd been so long since she last heard her native tongue that she'd all but forgotten it.

Along with the sound of his accent. That was why it'd seemed so familiar.

No wonder she'd liked hearing it. It made his voice seem even deeper.

Sexier.

And that explained why Eve was so drawn to him.

Every bit as tall and muscular as Jedi, he had long, white blond hair. Like hers. Only his was braided down his back, in the fashion of all high-ranking League assassins.

A rank doubly confirmed by his black battlesuit as all lower ranking assassins wore maroon uniforms. To earn a flat black meant that this man had personally murdered over two hundred people at the League's callous command. And half of those lives would have been decorated kills, meaning that they were either other League members or high-ranking political officers.

Scratch that . . .

Her eyes widened as she saw his sleeves in the faint light. Each one held a line of crowned daggers embroidered in blood red. The same blood red piping that marked his collar. There was absolutely no mistaking this man's rank. He was a First Rank Command Assassin.

A high commander. The so-called Top Ass.

And that was terrifying beyond all reason as less than one percent of League assassins were able to obtain his rank. A rank that meant he'd personally taken the lives of over five hundred assigned targets—with at least one hundred of them having been fully trained assassins.

Her stomach lurched at the very thought of what this man was capable of.

To call him deadly was an understatement. Yet Eve seemed perfectly at ease with someone who could kill them all and sleep like a baby.

Not that she blamed her. The man was gorgeous. His features were chiseled and harsh. As if the gods had wanted a perfect masculine specimen for this elite killing machine. Like cuddling up with a rabid lorina. A beautiful wild cat that could lick your hand one second, then rip your arm off the next.

In direct violation of League protocol and rules, Eve pulled the opaque sunglasses from his face. Assassins wore them so that no one would be able to tell where they were looking, or who they were targeting.

Dakari also had a feeling that they were required to wear them in order to look more intimidating, because without them, he appeared almost kind and good-spirited.

Indeed, he had a pair of eyes that were the clearest, most vibrant shade of cool steel . . .

Eyes that had haunted her since the last time she'd gazed into them.

I'll always protect you. Don't worry, Dakaboo. I've got you.

"Jinx?" Dakari choked on the name as it lodged itself in her throat. She was too afraid to speak it in case she was wrong and that somehow her eyes were deceiving her in the dim light.

He nodded.

A sob broke as she rushed forward to embrace the

brother she'd assumed for all these years was dead. Just like the rest of their family.

How could he be alive?

And an assassin?

"Um, hate to break up the family reunion, but we're not clear yet."

Jinx tightened his arms around her. "Tweedle's right. We need to hurry."

Dakari slapped his arm as he let her go. "Damn you! Why didn't you tell me you were alive? Why did you let me think you dead for all these years?"

He gestured at the League uniform he wore. "You'll be killed if they find out you survived. Or I will be."

Because assassins weren't allowed any weaknesses. If the League ever learned of any, it was instantly removed.

Should an assassin become maimed or unable to fulfill his or her role, they were executed. Plain and simple. There was no such thing as a retired assassin.

Retirement for them meant death.

They weren't allowed any kind of attachment or family. No friends.

Agents of death, their jobs were to be soulless monsters sent out to terrify and intimidate everyone in the universe.

She had no idea what they'd done to her brother to turn him into such a creature, and honestly, she didn't want to know. She'd heard enough stories about their brutal training. Most assassins never survived to wear any uniform at all.

Jinx had risen up through all their ranks . . .

That took more than just luck. It took ruthless skill and unbelievable intelligence.

Most of all, it took his soul.

Tears filled her eyes as she glanced to the name on his uniform. "Shadowborne?"

He swallowed hard. "I would never dishonor our parents by using their name for what I do. Tibon sent me to my death, but I was reborn in the shadows as the monster he only thinks he is."

Eve laughed bitterly. "Yeah, if payback's a bitch and revenge is sweet, then I must be the sweetest bitch you'll ever meet."

"Fuck that," Jedi said. "Payback takes way too long. I'd rather beat the shit out of them myself as soon as they need it. I swear, karma's a bitch asleep at the con, most of the time."

Jayne nodded. "Yeah, I got a long list of names karma's missed."

Dakari more than understood their feelings. She'd like to lay hands on Tibon right now and hand deliver to him her own justice that was decades overdue.

But she didn't want to think about him at the moment. Her real brother was much more important. "How did you survive?"

"Piss and venom, little sister." He winked at her. "Rule one. If you're going to make an enemy of someone who used to love you and attack him in the middle of the night when his guard's down, then you better make damn sure he doesn't survive." Jinx stroked her pale hair like he used to do when they kids.

"I don't understand."

"You were the one and only thing that was keeping Tobin alive. So long as he kept you safe, I was willing to sit back and let karma have him. Now . . ." He kissed her on the forehead and gently handed her off to Eve. "You know what to do."

Eve nodded. "You stay safe, my shadow."

"Don't worry. I know if I do something stupid, you'll punish me by sending Jed in after me."

Jayne laughed.

Jedi shook his head. "You only find it funny because your sister doesn't make you go fetch her idiot when he's doing something profoundly dangerous."

Jinx gave him a dry, annoyed glare. "Oh, for the number of times I have to whisper to myself . . . you're not worth a death sentence."

Jedi laughed. "Love you, too, big guy." Stepping forward, he hugged Jinx.

Dakari didn't miss the true affection they had for each other. Jinx was as much a part of their motley family as Jedi was.

He clapped Jedi on the arm. "Take care of my ladies."

"Will do, Top Ass."

Eve returned the sunglasses to his hand, then kissed him. "Remember your promise."

"I won't make you cry."

But the way they clung to each other brought tears to Dakari's eyes. There was no missing how much they loved each other.

Damn the League and Tobin for keeping them apart. The League would never let Jinx go and if anyone ever found out about Eve, they'd kill them both.

For that matter, Jinx would be killed if they ever learned he'd helped her. Which was why he took a moment to scan outside the door and listen in on the others.

As he started to leave, Dakari caught his arm. "Will I see you again?"

He covered her hand with his and smiled, then

glanced to Eve. "I'm always with you, Dakaboo I told you that. No one will ever hurt you on my watch."

Then he was gone so fast and silently that she could barely process it. Swallowed by the shadows he'd named himself after.

"Remember, Jinx!" Eve called out in a low tone. "When I asked, 'How stupid can you be?' It wasn't meant to be a personal challenge!"

A low laugh answered them from the darkness.

"You better stay safe," Eve growled.

With a deep sigh, she offered Dakari a smile. "Come on, princess. Time to find you safe place to stay."

Yeah, but there was no such place for her. Not anymore. "They'll be coming for me. It's a League contract. They won't rest until I'm dead."

"And that's your brother at your back. He'll make sure that you're cleared."

Dakari stared in the direction where Jinx had vanished. "You really think so?"

Eve nodded. "Your brother is just like me. How far will I go to protect what I love? All the way. Rain hell down on me and I will return it with interest. It's what makes him so lethal at what he does.

"And my sister," Jayne added. "We don't call her Eve of Rage for nothing."

Dakari scowled. "I thought she was known as Eve of Destruction."

Eve smirked. "You're both wrong. I'm Eve of Shadow's."

J

inx paused as he saw his half-brother sitting at the desk that had once belonged to their father. No sooner had Tobin slaughtered Jinx's parents and sold him off to the League thinking they'd massacre him before he hit puberty than Tobin had moved himself right in and taken over as if this was his right.

How sickening could one man be? To destroy those who had never harmed him. Those who had loved and cared for him, given him any and everything he'd ever wanted. Even before he asked for it.

And for what? Pride? Greed?

Stupidity?

Jealousy?

Jinx still didn't understand what had caused his brother to snap and lash out at the entire family in such a hate-filled rage.

Nine years older than Jinx, Tobin had thought himself their father's key advisor and helper. With lies and subtle manipulation, he'd isolated their father from everyone around him, including his own wife, Jinx's mother.

Tobin's worst fear had been that Jinx would one day replace him in his father's heart, or that Jinx's mother might break the spell he held over their father. That Jinx and Dakari might somehow take a cred from his greedy, slimy palm before he could spend all of their father's money.

And yet for all his greed and insistence that he was smarter than everyone else in the universe, including their father, within a year of their father's death, Tobin had driven their once rich and thriving empire into bankruptcy. That was just how stupid and delusional

Tobin had been about his "skills." It wasn't enough that he lied to everyone around him, he'd also lied to himself. Convinced himself that he could run their empire just as easily as their father had.

Now Eufora was one of the poorest, rundown districts in the Nine Worlds. They were reliant on loans and charity from other governments just to function. And it was minimal functioning at that.

Their father would weep to see the damage Tobin had wrought on his beloved empire. Perhaps it was best that he was dead, after all.

Too bad Tobin wasn't man enough to kill himself and do them all a favor.

As if anyone would ever miss so worthless a piece of shit.

But then cowards never did anyone for favor, except themselves.

Useless from beginning to end.

Tobin's "bright" answer for reinvigorating what he'd destroyed had been a rich, political marriage for Dakari to a man older than their father. His way of saving his ass, without having any regard for her or anyone else. Then when she'd refused to be his pawn, Tobin had put out a hit on her, thinking he could at least have the money from her life insurance.

His second mistake.

Funny how the ghosts of the past always came home to roost. *We are all the architects of our own demise.* His father's favorite quote.

Too bad Tobin hadn't remembered that.

His father had created his own death by spoiling a brat and praising him when he should have kicked Tobin in the ass and to the curb. Gereon Tievel should never have allowed Tobin to think or believe for one instant that he was something that he wasn't. That he actually had a single functioning brain cell in his head.

Now . . .

Jinx skirted past the bed where Tobin had a woman chained to it. Naked and alone for the moment, she lay with a pillow to her face so that she could muffle her sobs. Her back was covered with bruises and vicious handprints.

Disgusted by his brother's perversions, he wanted to free her, but better to leave her there so that no one could accuse her of his brother's death. Not that it wouldn't be justified.

Still, the poor woman had obviously been punished enough at Tobin's hands. She didn't need to suffer because of his death that was too long overdue.

Silent as the shadows he'd named himself after, Jinx crept into the room where his brother sat alone in his infinite misery, drinking and imbibing the drugs that used to make their father have to bail him out of jail.

Dressed in a bathrobe that he'd pulled over his naked body, but hadn't bothered to belt, Tobin looked exactly like the aged piece of miserable shit he was. His thinning hair had gone stark white and his face appeared much older than his years.

Be careful what you court as your companion, my son, for you will one day wear it for all the world to see. The body rots from the inside out, and your sins will devour your soul. Eventually, those sins will find themselves on the surface and the lines on your face will mark all the evil you've done. People will see and know exactly who and what you really are.

How weird that he'd only had a meager eleven years with his father and yet he remembered his wisdom so well. Meanwhile Tobin had been lucky enough to have him for twenty years and seemed to have forgotten everything.

Maybe evil made people stupid as well as blind.

It certainly made them twisted. And Jinx couldn't help but sneer as Tobin laughed at the video he'd taped of himself abusing the poor woman who was in his bedroom.

I should have done this years ago.

But an unsanctioned League hit against any political target could get him killed.

Then again, breathing while being a slave to the League could get him killed.

What good were his skills if he didn't use them to take out the trash once in a while? Let them come for him if they must.

Let his defiance redeem him.

"Is she dead yet?"

Jinx froze as he realized Tobin was on his comm, talking to someone.

"They're still hunting the little bitch. I swear, she has more lives than a lorina." That was Jessel's voice, Tobin's half-sister. While Jinx and Tobin shared a father, Jessel and Tobin shared a mother.

He remembered the snotty bitch from their childhood. With frizzy brown hair and a hateful smirk that made everyone want to slap her within ten minutes of meeting her, she'd been born resentful.

For reasons no one had ever understood, Tobin's mother used to send her to their home to visit with them any chance she could. Personally, he'd always thought it was to get back at his father and mother.

Surely there was no greater hell than being forced to tolerate Jessel's whiny, incessant complaints and insults.

But like a fool, his father had allowed it. Jinx had

never understood his father's tolerance, and especially not his mother's. But then Samara Tievel had been kind-hearted to the end, especially when it came to children. Both his parents had felt sorry for Jessel and Tobin. They'd thought them harmless and had wanted to help. To give them a better life.

How had their kindness been repaid?

Tobin had murdered them in front of the one son who had loved his father and worshiped his mother.

That horrific memory had lived in Jinx's heart every day of his life and every nightmare of his sleep. It was what had turned him into the monster the League craved and what gave him no mercy on anyone.

I am the hell you fear. Pray to your god that they never release me. That had been the promise Jinx had made to himself every single minute of his League training. *If I survive, I will pay my debt in full.*

Today it came due.

"Yeah, well, the League will get her, and she won't be our problem anymore. While her insurance isn't as high as the marriage would have been, it'll be enough to make us happy."

"Good. I need a new pair of shoes." Jessel laughed.

Jinx saw red.

But he pushed his anger down.

This wasn't about anger. It was payback.

Besides, Jessel was close in age to Dakari. Genetically close, too . . .

The rest could be forged, especially by a League high commander.

Keep talking, bitch.

And she did.

With every second that passed, Jinx pressed his hand harder over his forearm. Beneath his sleeve was the tattoo he'd gotten long ago to remind himself that he'd been fighting every day of his life since he was a child.

Not a Survivor.

A Warrior.

It wasn't over when he lost. It was over when he died.

And that wasn't today. So long as he lived, he would battle and may the gods help anyone who stood in front of him as an opponent.

Tobin disconnected his call with his sister and rose to his feet. Turning, he froze the instant he saw Jinx in the shadows. "Hope you got good news."

"I do."

Tobin let out a relieved breath. "She's dead?"

Jinx fought his urge to sneer. How pathetic that Dakari had been such a small child when last she'd seen him and yet she'd recognized him instantly.

He was the spitting image of his father and yet this bastard didn't see the resemblance at all.

Maybe it was the drink or drugs. But Jinx wasn't willing to be that kind. More like it was Tobin's rank stupidity. Or simple lack of regard for anyone other than himself.

Even the father he'd butchered in front of his eleven-year-old brother. Because no one mattered in the world, except Tobin and what Tobin wanted. Everyone else was expendable.

"You know, Tobin, the Euforians have an old saying. The axe forgets what the tree remembers."

"What?"

He shook his head. "Don't remember that one, huh? Then about, nothing good will ever happen to those who break their oaths." He pulled his sunglasses from his eyes. "Do you remember the oath you once made to me?"

Tobin went pale as he finally realized who he was talking to. "Uh ... um ..."

"You promised me that you would take care of Dakari. Nothing would happen to her. So long as you held that vow, I withheld my blade." Jinx pulled out his sacred League seax. Every assassin had their one weapon of choice.

Their favorite means of execution.

This long, black razor-sharp dagger was his.

"You're supposed to be dead!" Tobin tried to run, then tripped and fell.

"And you were never supposed to rule my father's empire. But this is the Ichidian universe, Tobin. Every life has a price."

Too bad Tobin's was worthless.

Without blinking or hesitating, Jinx ended his brother just as he'd been taught. Taught because Tobin had sold him to the League to be used as a target for assassins to practice their lethal skills on. The idea was to hand-feed them a child so that they could learn not to feel compassion.

To kill indiscriminately, regardless of age or size.

They had failed their assignments.

He had not. For that was the one rule of his species. Don't die.

I am not survivor.

I'm a warrior.

And tonight, the tree felled the axe, and Jinx kept his oath to his sister.

Dakari would be forever safe as soon as he paid Jessel a visit ...

Family was all. Let them rain their hell down on him if they must. But it wouldn't end well for them if they tried. For he was no longer a frightened little boy sold to the League to die. He was a well-honed killing machine who had no compassion for anyone dumb enough to come after him, or the tiny handful of people he cared about.

My silence isn't weakness.

It only means the beast inside me is asleep. Not dead.

THE NEIGHBORS

1

"I think there's something wrong with our neighbors." Jamie stepped back from the window to frown at his mom. "Have you seen them?"

"Just when the Thompsons moved in a few months ago and Teresa gave me her number."

"But not since, right?"

With long blond hair and bright green eyes that matched his, his mom picked up his little sister's backpack and set it on the table near him. "Teresa said that her husband's an international antique dealer. He travels a lot and keeps weird hours whenever he works from home."

Jamie moved to sit down at the table to do his homework. "I'm telling you, Ma, there's something really, really off about them."

"Stop reading all those horror novels and watching those creepy movies and TV shows. No more Stephen King. It's all making you paranoid."

Maybe, but still . . .

Jamie had a bad feeling that wouldn't go away. Unsettled, he watched as his mom collected Matilda's toys and sighed from exhaustion.

It'd been hard for all of them over the last few

months since his dad had been killed while off on a "business" trip.

As Jamie opened his chemistry book, a motion outside caught his attention. Frowning, he slid out of his chair to get a closer look.

He gaped at the sight of his neighbor carrying a strange-shaped baggie out of his detached garage and tossing it into the trunk of his car . . . which, now that he thought about it, was never parked in the garage.

Neither was Teresa's.

His neighbor struggled with the weight and odd shape of whatever was in that bag.

Was it a body?

C'mon, dude. Don't be stupid. It's not a body.

But Jamie had seen plenty of horror movies where they moved corpses, and that was what it looked like. It didn't even bend right.

Definitely rigamortis.

"James? What are you doing?"

He pulled back to see his mom glaring at him. "Being my usual delusional self. You?"

"Wondering what I got into while pregnant that caused your brain damage. Must have been those lead paint chips I craved."

"Ha, ha." He returned to his homework, but as he tried to focus on chemistry, he couldn't get his mind off what he'd just seen.

The way his neighbor had carried that bag . . .

It had to be a body.

Unable to concentrate, he got up to look outside again. The moment he did, he saw his neighbor's wife, Teresa, with a huge white bucket that held some kind of thick red liquid she was spreading around the driveway.

Red?

Water?

Nah, man. It was too thick for water. Looked like blood. Diluted maybe, but definitely hemoglobin-like substance.

He started to call for his mom, but the moment he opened his mouth, Teresa looked up and caught sight of him in the window.

Terrified and shaking, he quickly hit the deck on his belly.

Oh God, she saw me!

What was he going to do? *I know what blood looks like.* Even diluted. And that had been blood she'd been dumping.

Maybe she's a taxidermist.

Yeah, right.

"Jamie?"

He flinched at his sister's call. Crawling across the floor, he didn't get up until he was in the hallway. "What'cha need, Matty?"

With honey-blond curls and bright blue eyes, his little sister stared up at him from the couch. "Can you come help me? I can't get the TV on the right channel."

"Sure." He moved toward her to check it out. The battery on the remote was low.

After changing it for her, he returned to the living room to put it on the kids channel she preferred, then froze as he heard the news.

"Another body was found near Miller's Pond. Mutilated. The headless remains were burned beyond recognition. At this time, the authorities are investigating every lead. So far, they're at a loss over this horrific crime that appears to be related to a set of six murders over the last four months."

Jamie was frozen to the spot as he heard those words.

Six murders.

Four months.

"Give me that!" Matilda jerked the remote from his hand and changed channels.

Sick to his stomach, Jamie bit his lip. Now that he thought about it, those murders had only started after the Thompsons had moved in.

Six months ago. Just a few weeks after his father had been killed outside of Memphis.

Weird.

It's nothing, dumb ass. Get back to your chemistry.

Yeah, but what if . . .

"Jamie?"

He turned at his mother's irate tone that usually denoted one bad habit he had. "I put the seat down!"

She growled at him. "It's not the toilet seat. I just got a call from Teresa. Are you spying on her?"

Well, yeah, but he wasn't dumb enough to give her the truth with that tone of voice. "No."

Hands on hips, she glared at him. "You better not be! She said she's going to call the cops and report you for stalking if you do it again."

"'Cause I was looking out the window of my house? Really? When did that become a crime?"

"Don't get smart with me, boy. Now do your homework."

Grousing under his breath, Jamie returned to his book, but not before he called his best friend.

By the time he'd finished his assignment, Ed was at his back door with an evil grin on his nerdy little face. Barely five-foot-three, Ed wasn't the most intimidating person on the planet, but he was one hell of an opponent on any science or math bowl team.

"So, you think your neighbors are weird."

"Shh." Jamie looked over his shoulder to make sure his mom wasn't there before he pushed Ed out onto the back stoop. "Yeah. There's something not right. You feel up to some snooping?"

"Always. It's what I do best. . . . Only time my compact body mass comes in handy."

Ignoring his mini-tirade, Jamie turned the back light off and crouched low as he made his way from the porch to the grass. Like a military assault squad, they headed across his back yard, toward the Thompson's.

Halfway to the Thompson garage, Ed pulled back with a frown.

"What?" Jamie whispered.

Blanching, Ed held his hand up for him to see. "It's blood." He looked around. "The ground's saturated with it."

Sick to his stomach, Jamie lifted his hands to see them stained red. Just like Ed's. "Is it human?"

"How would I know? Blood's blood. And this is definitely blood." Ed's eyes widened. "You think they're the serial killers the cops are looking for?"

"I don't know."

Biting his lip, Jamie moved toward the detached two-car garage to look for clues. It took several minutes to jimmy the lock.

As silent as the grave, he and Ed moved into the small building that was covered in plastic.

Like some serial killer's lair.

Ed stepped closer to him. "We need to get out of here and call the cops."

"Not without some evidence."

"Yeah, no, I've seen this movie. Nerdy white boy dies first. I'm out of here."

He grabbed Ed's arm as his eyes adjusted to the darkness. "Hold on a minute."

Jamie went to the workbench where someone had left a map of their small Mississippi town and a card case.

A card case that held driver's licenses.

What the hell?

Opening it, Jamie saw men and women from all over the country. *What kind of . . .*

His thoughts scattered as he saw his dad's license there.

Why would they have his dad's license?

Confused and terrified, Jamie looked back at the map that had his house and those of every family in town marked with a red highlighter.

"Jamie," Ed snarled between clenched teeth. "I hear something."

As they started back for the window, Jamie froze at the sight of a mirrored wall.

Footsteps moved closer.

Ed ran for the window with Jamie one step behind him. They were both sweating and shaking by the time they were outside the garage. But as soon as their feet were on the ground, headlights lit up the entire yard.

They were trapped.

If they tried to get back to Jamie's house, they'd be seen for sure.

With no other course of action, Jamie crouched under the open window and listened as the driver turned the car off and got out. Footsteps echoed as the driver walked into the garage.

"Hey, hon?" Mr. Thompson called out. "Have you been messing in the garage again?"

Lights came on in the house an instant before

Teresa walked the short distance to the garage. "What now, Bob?"

Ed ran for Jamie's house while Jamie stayed behind. Rising slowly, he peeked in through the window to see the Thompsons standing in the center of their obvious kill zone.

"Someone's been flipping through my journal. Was that you?"

"No. I haven't been in here." She walked over to the mirror.

Jamie gasped at what he saw there.

Oh shit! I knew it!

He lifted his phone and quickly snapped a photo of her, then he did what Ed had done. He scampered across the lawn as fast as he could. Running into his house, he slammed the door and pulled down all the window blinds.

"Mom!"

Ed met him in the living room where he was holding on to Matilda for everything he was worth. "I thought those things were myths made up by teachers and parents to scare us."

"What?" his mom asked.

Jamie swallowed as his mother stared at them as if they were crazy. His breathing ragged, he held his phone out to his mom. "We've got to call the cops!"

"For what?"

"Our neighbors, Ma!" He showed her the picture of them standing in front of the mirror . . . casting a reflection. "They're humans . . . slayers. And they're here to destroy our colony!"

ALSO BY SHERRILYN KENYON
(LISTED IN CORRECT READING ORDER)

ᛞARK-HUNTER®

SherrilynKenyon.com

ABOUT THE AUTHOR

Defying all odds is what #1 New York Times and international bestselling author Sherrilyn Kenyon does best. Rising from extreme poverty as a child that culminated in being a homeless mother with an infant, she has become one of the most popular and influential authors in the world (in both adult and young adult fiction), with dedicated legions of fans known as Paladins–thousands of whom proudly sport tattoos from her numerous genre-defying series.

Since her first book debuted in 1993 while she was still in college, she has placed more than 80 novels on the New York Times list in all formats and genres, including manga and graphic novels, and has more than 70 million books in print worldwide. Her current series include: Dark-Hunters®, Chronicles of Nick®, Deadman's Cross™, Black Hat Society™, Nevermore™, Silent Swans™, Lords of Avalon® and The League®.

Over the years, her Lords of Avalon® novels have been adapted by Marvel, and her Dark-Hunters® and Chronicles of Nick® are New York Times bestselling manga and comics and are #1 bestselling adult coloring books.

Join her and her Paladins online at QueenofAll-Shadows.com and www.facebook.com/mysherrilyn.